Sophie's Snail

OTHER STORIES BY DICK KING-SMITH:

Sophie's Snail

DICK KING-SMITH

Illustrated by Hannah Shaw

WALKER
BOOKS

This edition published 2015

2 4 6 8 10 9 7 5 3 1

Text © 1988 Fox Busters Ltd
Illustrations © 2015 Hannah Shaw

The right of Dick King-Smith and Hannah Shaw to be identified
as author and illustrator respectively of this work has been
asserted by them in accordance with the Copyright,
Designs and Patents Act 1988

This book has been typeset in ITC Veljovic

Printed and bound in Great Britain by Clays Ltd, St Ives plc

British Library Cataloguing in Publication Data:
a catalogue record for this book is available from the British Library

ISBN 978-1-4063-4305-2

www.walker.co.uk

Contents

One Very Small Foot

"What animal has got only one foot?" said the children's father. "I bet you can't tell me."

"I can!" said Matthew and Mark with one voice. As well as looking exactly alike, the twins nearly always said exactly the same thing at exactly the same time. Matthew was ten minutes older than Mark, but after that there had never been the slightest difference between them.

"Go on then," said their father. "Tell me. What animal's got only one foot?"

"A chicken standing on one leg!" they said.

"That's silly," said Sophie seriously.

Sophie was four, a couple of years younger than her brothers.

"That's silly," she said. "It would still have a foot on the other leg. Anyway, Daddy, there isn't really an animal that's only got one foot, is there?"

"Yes, there is, Sophie."

"What?"

"A snail. Every snail has a big flat sticky muscle under it that it travels along on. That's called its foot. Next time you see a snail crawling along, pick it up carefully and turn it over, and you'll see. There are loads in the garden."

8

"Come on! Let's find one!"
said Matthew to Mark and Mark to
Matthew at the same time.

"Wait for me," said Sophie. But they
didn't, so she plodded after them.

When she caught up with the twins
in a far corner of the garden, each was
examining the underside of a large snail.
Sophie was not surprised to see that the
snails were also obviously twins: the
same size, the same shape, the same
striped greeny-browny colour.

"I know!" said Matthew.

"I know what you're going to say!" said Mark.

"Let's have a snail race!" they said.

"How are you going to tell them apart?" said Sophie.

"I know!" said Mark.

"I know what you're going to say!" said Matthew.

"Fetch us a felt pen, Sophie," they said.

"What are you going to do?" asked Sophie when she came back with a red felt pen.

"Put my initial on my snail," said Mark and Matthew together.

"But you've got the same initial."

The boys looked at each other.

"I know!" they said.

"I know what you're going to say,"

said Sophie, and she plodded off again. She came back with a blue felt pen.

After a moment, "Ready?" said Matthew, holding up his snail with a big red **M** on its shell, and at the same instant, "Ready?" said Mark, holding up his snail with a big blue **M**.

"Wait for me," said Sophie. "I haven't got a snail yet." But already the twins had set their twin snails side by side on the path that ran between the edge of the lawn and the flowerbed. The path was made of big oval flagstones, and they chose the largest one, perhaps a metre long. The far end of the flagstone was to be the winning post.

"Ready, steady, go!" they shouted.

Sophie plodded off. "I'll beat them," she said. She was small but very determined.

Behind the first stone she moved, almost as though it had been waiting for her, was a snail. It was as different as possible from Red **M** and Blue **M**. It was very little, no bigger than Sophie's middle fingernail, and it was a lovely buttercup yellow.

As she watched, it stretched out its head, poked out its two horns and began to crawl, very slowly. It had a most intelligent face, Sophie thought. She picked it up carefully and turned it over.

"What a very small-sized shoe you would take, my dear," she said. "I don't know whether you can win a race but you are very beautiful. You shall be my snail."

"Who won?" she said
to Matthew and Mark
when she returned.

"They didn't go the
right way," they both said.

"But mine went furthest,"
they both said.

"No, it didn't," they both
said.

They picked up their snails and put
them side by side once more.

"Wait for me," Sophie said, and she put
down the little yellow snail. It looked
very small beside the others.

"Just look at Sophie's snail!" hooted the twins, but this time when they shouted "Ready, steady, go!" neither Red **M** nor Blue **M** would move. They stayed stubbornly inside their shells and took not the slightest notice of their owners' cries of encouragement.

Sophie's snail plodded off.

It was small but very determined, and Sophie lay on the grass beside the path and watched it putting its best foot forward.

After half
an hour, it
reached the
winning post.
Sophie jumped
up. "Mine's the winner!" she cried,
but there was no one to hear.

16

The twins had become bored with snail-racing at exactly the same time and gone away. Red **M** and Blue **M** had gone away too, into the forest of the flowerbed. Only Sophie's snail kept stoutly on, while the straight silvery trail it had left glistened in the sunshine.

Sophie knelt down and carefully put her hand flat in front of the little yellow creature. It crawled solemnly onto it.

"You have such an intelligent look, my dear," said Sophie.

"What *have* you got in your hand, Sophie?" said her mother at tea-time.

"It's Sophie's snail!" chorused Matthew and Mark.

"Put it straight out in the garden," said the children's mother.

"No," said Sophie in a small but determined voice.

Her mother looked at her, sighed, picked up a box of matches, emptied the matches out and gave Sophie the empty box.

"Put it in there till after tea," she said, "and go and wash your hands."

*   *   *

All that evening Sophie played with her snail. When it was bedtime and she was ready to wash and do her teeth, she put the snail carefully on the flat rim of the washbasin.

Then (as she always did) she filled the basin with warm water right up to the overflow and washed her face and hands. The snail did not move, though it appeared to be watching.

19

Then (as she always did) she brushed her teeth very hard, making a lot of froth in her mouth and spitting the bubbly blobs of toothpaste out on top of the rather dirty water. She always liked doing this. The toothpaste blobs made strange shapes on the surface of the water, often like a map of the world. Tonight there was a big white Africa at one side of the basin.

Then (as she always did) she pulled the plug out, but as she turned to dry her hands the sleeve of her dressing gown scuffed the rim of the basin. Right into the middle of disappearing Africa fell a small yellow shape, and then the last of the whirlpooling frothing water disappeared

down the plug hole, leaving the
basin quite empty.

Sophie plodded
down the stairs.

"My snail's gone down the plug
hole," she said in a very quiet voice.

"You couldn't have kept it, you know,"
said her father gently. "It would have died
anyway without its natural food."

"Next time you find one," said her
mother, "just leave it in the garden. There
are lots of other snails there, just as nice."

"Not as nice as my snail," said Sophie.
She looked so unhappy that for once the
twins said different things, in an effort to
comfort her.

"'Spect it died quickly," said Matthew.

"Sure to be drowned by now," said
Mark.

*　*　*

Try as she would, Sophie could not stop
herself thinking about what happened
to you if you went down a plug hole. She
lay in bed and thought about the twins
washing their hands in the basin and
brushing their teeth, and then later on,
Mum and Dad doing the same. All that
water would be washing the body of her
snail farther and farther away, down the
drain into the sewer, down the sewer into
the river, down the river into the sea.

When at last she slept, she dreamed
that she was walking by the seaside, and
there she saw, washed up on the beach, a
familiar little yellow shape. But when she
ran and picked it up, it had no head, no
horns, no foot. It was just an empty snail
shell.

Sophie woke early with the feeling that something awful had happened, and then she remembered what it was.

She plodded along to the bathroom and looked over the rim of the washbasin at the round plug hole with its metal grating meant to stop things going down it.

"But you were too small," she said.

Leaning over as far as she could reach, she stared sadly into the black depths of the plug hole. And as she stared, suddenly two little horns poked up through the grating, and then a head, and then a shell no bigger than her middle fingernail, a shell that was a lovely buttercup yellow.

Very carefully Sophie reached out and picked up her small determined snail.

Very quietly she plodded down the stairs and opened the back door and went out into the garden and crossed the dewy lawn.

Very gently, at the exact spot she had found it, she put her snail down and watched it slowly move away on its very small foot.

"Goodbye, my dear," said Sophie. "I hope we meet again." And then she sat happily on the wet grass watching, till at last there was nothing more to be seen of Sophie's snail.

Farm Munny

"When I grow up," said Sophie at
breakfast time, "I'm going to be a farmer."

"You can't," said the twins.

"Why not?"

"Farmers are men," they said.

"Well," said Sophie, "I'm going to be a
lady farmer. So there."

Her father looked at her over the top of
his newspaper.

"I'm sure you are, Sophie," he said. "I'm
sure you could do anything you were

determined to do. But you'd need an awful lot of money. Suppose you wanted to be a dairy farmer. Just think how much a big herd of cows would cost."

"I wouldn't have a big herd of cows," said Sophie.

"How many would you have?" asked Mark.

"I'd just have one cow, called Blossom."

"Well then, you wouldn't have much milk to sell," said her father.

"I wouldn't have *any* milk to sell," said Sophie.

"Why not?" asked Matthew.

"I should drink it all. I like milk."

She held out her glass.

"Can I have some more please, Mum?" she said.

"I don't really think," said her mother, "that you could call yourself a farmer..."

"A lady farmer," said the twins.

"...if the only thing you had was one cow."

"It wouldn't be the only thing," Sophie said. "I'd have two hens, called April and May."

"Why April?" said Matthew.

"Why May?" said Mark.

"Because they're nice months. And these would be nice hens."

"You wouldn't have many eggs to sell," said her father.

"I wouldn't have *any* eggs to sell," said Sophie.

"Because you'd eat them all," said Mark.

"Because you like eggs," said Matthew.

"I do," said Sophie. "I'm very fond of eggs."

She looked at the boiled egg that her mother had just put in front of her. Sophie had her own special blue egg cup with her name written on it in white letters. The egg was a big brown one.

"Excuse me, my dear," said Sophie, and she tapped it gently with her spoon. "I don't think it hurts them," she said.

Matthew and Mark looked at each other, and each rolled his eyes upwards and raised his eyebrows and tapped his forehead with one finger.

"What other animals will you keep?" said Sophie's father.

"A pony."

"What kind of pony?"

"A Shetland pony. I like Shetland ponies."

"But Sophie," said her mother, "don't you think a Shetland pony will be rather small for you when you're a grown-up lady farmer? I mean, your legs will drag along the ground."

"I shan't ride it," said Sophie. "It'll just be a pet. I shall call it Shorty."

"What other pets will you keep?"

"Just a pig."

"Pigs aren't pets," said the twins.

"Measles will be."

"Why Measles?"

"Because he'll be a spotty pig, of course," said Sophie, looking scornfully at her brothers. "You've got no imagination, you two haven't."

She scraped the last bits out of her boiled egg and then turned it upside down on top of the egg cup so that it looked untouched.

"There you are, my dear," she said. "Good as new."

"Let me see if I've got it right," said her father. "When you're a lady farmer, you're going to keep a cow and two hens and a pony and a pig. Am I right?"

"Yes," said Sophie. "And I shall grow a little field of corn."

"What for?" said Matthew and Mark.

"Cornflakes, of course," said Sophie. "Don't they teach you anything at school?"

"But what are you going to live on?" asked her father.

"Milk and eggs and cornflakes. I'm very fond of all those."

"No, no, I mean how are you going to manage? None of the animals – Blossom and April and May and Shorty and Measles – is going to earn you any money. And how will you afford to buy them in the first place?"

"I shall save up."

"But that will take you years and years and years," said the twins.

"I've got years and years and years," said Sophie. With that she got down from the table and plodded off.

"She'll never get enough money to be a lady farmer," said Matthew.

"Will she, Dad?" asked Mark.

"I wouldn't be too sure about that," said their father. "Your sister may be small but she is a very determined person."

So nobody was very surprised next morning when Sophie came in to breakfast carrying her piggy bank and placed it on the table.

On its side was stuck a notice, which said:

Farm munny
Thankyou
Sophie

Sophie's father put his hand in his pocket and took out a one pound coin and dropped it in. Her mother fetched her bag and added another.

Matthew and Mark looked at each other.

"I've only got 20p," said Matthew.

"Same here," said Mark.

"Every little helps," said Sophie.

Aunt Alice

The children's father looked up from the letter he was reading.

"It's from Aunt Alice," he said in rather a surprised voice. "She's coming to see us."

"Who's Aunt Alice?" asked the twins.

"She's Daddy's aunt," said their mother. "Or rather she's Grandpa's aunt, so she's Daddy's great-aunt."

"I've never seen a great aunt," Sophie said.

"Well, of course, she's more than that to

you three children. She's a great-great-aunt."

"Yikes!" said Sophie. "She must be *enormous*!"

"You'll soon be able to see," said her father. "She's asked herself to lunch next Sunday."

"Why haven't we seen her before?" asked Matthew and Mark.

"Because she lives about six hundred miles away, in the Highlands of Scotland."

"It's a long way to come for lunch," said Sophie.

"No, no, she's already down this way, staying in London for a few days."

The twins forgot almost at once about the coming visit of Great-Great-Aunt Alice, but Sophie didn't.

She wondered about the Highlands.

How did you get down from them? On a rope? Or a ladder?

She wondered about this great-great-aunt. How would she get to London? In a train? But she might be too big to get through the carriage door. In an aeroplane perhaps? Yes, that would be best, in one of those huge ones with fat tummies that you could put tanks and lorries and things inside. The plane could fly off the top of the Highlands and then, when it got to London, they could open the big doors at the back and this enormous aunt could walk out.

But when Sunday came, and the front door opened, it was a very small person who walked in. The top of her head, Sophie could see, didn't even come up to Daddy's shoulder.

"Now then, Aunt Al," Sophie's father said, "these are the twins, Matthew and Mark."

"How de do?" said Aunt Alice, and she shook each boy's hand in turn.

Although it wasn't always so, Matthew and Mark happened this day to be wearing exactly the same clothes.

"Like as two peas in a pod," said Aunt Alice. "Which is which?"

"I'm Matthew," said Matthew.

"I'm Mark," said Mark.

"I'm nearly ten minutes older," said Matthew.

"And I'm two years younger," said Sophie.

"Ah!" said Aunt Alice. "Now you must be Sophie." She took hold of Sophie's hand and held it, looking at her with

sharp blue eyes. She looked rather like a
bird, Sophie thought, with those bright
eyes and a thin beaky nose and hands
that were skinny and bony and curled
like a bird's claws.

"And how old are you, Sophie?" she said.

"I'm four," said Sophie. "How old are
you?"

"Sophie!" said her mother. "You can't
go asking things like that!"

"Why not?" said Sophie. "She
asked *me*, didn't you?"

"Quite right," said Aunt Alice.
"Load of rubbish, people not
wanting to tell
their age. I'm
eighty. And I'm
hungry as a hunter.
When's lunch?"

After lunch, Sophie and Aunt Alice sat on a swing-seat on the lawn. Sophie's parents were doing the washing-up and the twins were playing with a football at the far end of the garden.

Aunt Alice's small shoes just touched the ground, and she swung the seat gently back and forth. Sophie sat beside her, feet sticking straight out, and looked directly at the bird-face. I don't know about a great-great-aunt, she thought. Looks to me more like a small-small-aunt.

"What shall I call you?" she said.

"Same as everyone else does. Aunt Al. It's nice and short, like me."

"Are the Highlands very high, Aunt Al?" said Sophie.

"Quite high."

"And cold?"

"Quite cold."

"Lots of snow?"

"Masses, in winter."

"Polar bears?"

"No," said Aunt Alice. "But lots of lovely creatures, like golden eagles and blue hares and red deer."

They swung in silence for a while.

Then Sophie said, "It sounds nice. I wouldn't have bothered coming down off the top of the Highlands to go to London if I were you."

"I don't often. But there were a few things that I wanted to do."

"Like coming to lunch with us?"

"Of course. And doing some shopping. And seeing about my will."

"What's the matter with your Will?" said Sophie. "Is he ill?"

Aunt Alice gave a little chirp of amusement, but before she could answer, the twins came running up and stood side by side in front of her, grinning.

Sophie sighed.

She knew those identical grins.

She knew what was coming.

Still sighing, she wriggled down from the swing-seat and plodded off.

Aunt Alice looked at the two boys.

"Hello," she said.

"Hello," they said.

"Guess..." said Matthew.

"...which is which," said Mark.

"Bet you can't tell," they said. It was a game they never tired of playing. If the visitor guessed wrong anyway, well and good. But if the guess was right, if the visitor pointed at Matthew and said, "You're Matthew," he would reply, "Mark." And if Mark was correctly chosen, he would answer, "Matthew." So they always won.

Sophie did not approve of this.

"You tell lies," she said severely.

"No, we don't," they said. "We just say each other's name. That's not telling lies."

However, Sophie did not approve of telling tales, either, so she had never said anything. Still, she would not watch when

they played this game on people, but
always stumped off.

Aunt Alice looked at the grinning twins.

"Bet I can," she said.

She opened her bag and
took out her purse. From it
she took two pound coins.

"Tell you what," she said.
"If I'm wrong, you each get one of these."

"All right!" they cried eagerly.

Aunt Alice stared long and carefully
at each boy in turn, nodding her neat
head up and down as if she were a thrush
choosing between two worms. Then
suddenly, like a bird pecking, she said,
"Quick! Which of you's the older?" Before
he could stop himself, Matthew twitched
his mouth.

Aunt Alice looked at him poker-faced.

"You," she said deliberately, "are ...
Mark."

"No!" they both shouted delightedly.
"No! You're wrong!"

"Honestly?" said Aunt Alice.

"Honestly," they said.

"In that case, I'd better pay up."

When Matthew and Mark had run off
whooping and cheering, Sophie came
plodding back. She climbed on to the
swing-seat.

"I've just been guessing which twin
was which," Aunt Alice said.

"Huh!" said Sophie. She sighed.

"Whatever can you mean?" said Aunt
Alice.

Sophie looked very directly at her
great-great-aunt.

47

"Aunt Al," she said. "Can you keep a secret?"

"Sure thing."

"Sometimes one of them pretends to be the other."

"Disgraceful," said Aunt Alice. "What wicked boys."

"I don't know," said Sophie. "They're all right really. They just get overexcited."

They sat side by side, swinging gently. For some time neither spoke. Each was comfortable with the silence.

Then Sophie said, "Did you give them money?"

"Yes."

"They'll only spend it."

"Wouldn't you, if I gave you money?"

"No, I'd save it. I'm saving up for a farm."

"A toy one?"

"No, a real one."

"Whew! That'll take a long time."

"I expect it will," said Sophie.

Aunt Alice looked very directly at her great-great-niece.

"Sophie," she said. "Can you keep a secret?"

"Sure thing."

Aunt Alice took out her purse again.

"I gave the boys a pound each," she said, "but I'm going to give you two." And she did.

"Yikes!" said Sophie. "Thanks!"

"After all," said Aunt Alice with a grin, "it's not your fault that you're not twins."

Dawn

"What shall we do this morning, Matthew?" said Mark.

"I know!" said Matthew.

"I know what you're going to say!" said Mark.

"Let's go and play football!" they said.

"Mum!" they shouted. "We're going out to play football."

"Well, take Sophie with you."

"She doesn't much like football."

"You never ask her. Go and ask her

now." But when they found Sophie and asked her, she said she was too busy. So they went without her.

A little later Sophie's mother went out into the garden and found Sophie plodding round, peering into the flowerbeds as though searching for something. She was carrying a small yellow bucket.

"Why didn't you go with the twins?" her mother said.

"Too busy," grunted Sophie.

She bent down and picked up a spent matchstick and put it in her bucket.

"Oh, you are a good girl, Sophie," said her mother, "picking up Daddy's old matchsticks. Every time he smokes his pipe he uses dozens of matches to keep the wretched thing alight, and then he chucks the used ones all over the garden. But wouldn't you rather be playing with the others than just picking up matchsticks?"

"I'm not just picking up matchsticks," said Sophie severely. "I'm collecting food for all of my animals."

Sophie's mother went back to her housework shaking her head. She's getting to be a proper loner, she thought. Collecting food for her animals indeed! Whoever heard of animals eating wood! She lives in a world of her own. It's not good for her. I wish there was a girl of her own age for her to play with.

A couple of weeks later, Sophie's mother's wish was granted. A nearby house changed hands and the new people who moved in had a little girl who looked to be just about Sophie's age, a pretty little girl with golden hair done in bunches.

Sophie's mother lost no time in making contact.

"Sophie," she said one morning. "Those new people down the road have got a little girl."

"I know," said Sophie. "I've seen her. She wears frocks."

Sophie did not approve of frocks.

"She's called Dawn," said her mother.

"Yuk," said Sophie. She thrust her hands into the pockets of her old jeans and stumped off, shoulders hunched, the very picture of disapproval.

"I've asked them round this morning," her mother called after her. She turned to the twins. "You three children can play with Dawn while we're having coffee," she said.

"What time are they coming?" said Matthew.

"Eleven o'clock."

"We've got a football match," said Mark.

"Kick-off half past ten sharp," they said.

Dawn was wearing a green dress with bows on it, and long white socks, and smart red shoes. Her bunches were tied with green ribbon. She carried a little toy pony.

Dawn's mother raised her eyebrows just a tiny bit as Sophie was called up to be introduced.

Sophie was wearing an old blue jersey with her name written on it, and her old jeans, and her muddy wellies. Her dark hair looked as though she had just come through a hedge backwards. She carried her yellow bucket.

"Sophie," said her mother. "This is Dawn."

Dawn held out her toy pony. It was a bright pink pony with a long silvery mane and tail. It even had long silvery nylon eyelashes.

"This is Twinkletoes," she said. "He's my special favourite. But you can play with him if you like."

Sophie stared woodenly at Twinkletoes. It was plain from her expression that she did not approve of pink ponies.

"Yes, off you go and play," said Sophie's mother. "And, Sophie, you look after Dawn, there's a good girl."

Sophie stumped off with Dawn prancing beside her crying, "Gee-up, Twinkletoes! Gee-up, little pony!"

They came to the nearest flower-bed,
and Sophie began to hunt about.

"What are you looking for, Sophie?"
asked Dawn.

"Matchsticks," said Sophie shortly.

She found a couple and put them
in her bucket.

"Ugh!" said Dawn,
wrinkling her nose. "Nasty
old matchsticks! Whatever
do you want them for?"

"To feed my animals on," said Sophie.

Dawn laughed. "You are silly, Sophie,"
she said. "Matchsticks are made of wood.
Animals don't eat wood."

"Mine do," said Sophie.

"Isn't she silly, Twinkletoes?" said Dawn
to her pony. "You wouldn't eat dirty old
matchsticks, would you? You like nice

grass," and she pulled some from the lawn and held them against the pink muzzle.

"You're just pretending to feed it," said Sophie scornfully. "My animals are real. I'll show you."

At the bottom of the garden was an old potting-shed. Outside it, because they were too large to fit on the shelves, stood several very big flowerpots, upside down.

Carefully Sophie tipped one of the big pots over. Underneath it, on a bed of spent matchsticks, was a great army of woodlice.

"Good morning, my dears," said Sophie. "Here's two more nice juicy matchsticks for you."

"Ugh!" said Dawn, clasping Twinkletoes closely to her. "Horrible dirty creepy-crawlies!"

At that moment a large woodlouse detached itself from the mass and began to walk towards her feet.

Very deliberately, Dawn placed one of her smart red shoes on it and squashed it flat.

The yells from the bottom of the garden brought both mothers running. A dramatic scene met their eyes.

In front of the potting-shed a small, stocky figure was jumping solemnly, up and down, wellies together, on what had once been a bright pink pony with a silvery mane and tail but was now a dirty squashed lump.

"Sophie!" cried Sophie's mother.

"Dawn, darling!" cried Dawn's mother.

Waaaaa!!

"Waaaaaa!"
cried Dawn.
Sophie gave
one final stamp
on the battered body
of Twinkletoes, and
plodded off.

"Where's Sophie?"
asked the twins
when they came back from their game.

"She's in her room. She's been extremely
naughty."

"What did she do?"

"Never you mind."

"Where's Sophie?" asked her father
when he came back from work.

"She's in her room. She's been extremely
naughty."

"What did she do?"

"She completely ruined a toy belonging to the child of those new people down the road. Jumped on it. Squashed it."

"Why did she do that?"

"I don't know. I've asked her, but she won't answer."

"She'll answer me," Sophie's father said.

A few minutes later he came back.

"She won't," he said.

Even before Dawn's mother had said a frosty goodbye and taken her yelling daughter away, Sophie had gone straight to her room. She judged it better to go to her room than to be sent there. She sat on the side of her bed, thinking sadly of the death of the woodlouse. After a while the sad thoughts became glad ones.

Dawn had paid for that! She would have to pay too, out of her Farm Money, but it would be worth it!

At bedtime the twins looked in on Sophie. They sat on the end of her bed, Matthew on one side and Mark on the other.

"What did you do?" they said.

"I busted Dawn's toy," said Sophie. "I jumped on it."

"Why?" said Mark.

"She squashed one of my woodlouses," said Sophie.

"Squashed it dead?" said Matthew.

"Yes."

"What a beastly girl," they said.

"And the toy was a horrible pink pony called Twinkletoes."

"Yuk!" they said.

"You were right to jump on it," said Matthew.

"You should have jumped on her, too," said Mark.

"Did you tell Mum and Dad what she did?" they asked.

"No," said Sophie. "They'd only say 'I'm sure she didn't mean to' or 'It was only a woodlouse after all'."

A little later Sophie's mother and father came in. They sat on the end of Sophie's bed, one on each side.

"You know, Sophie," said her father, "you simply can't go breaking other children's toys."

"I can," said Sophie. "I just have."

"You'll have to say you're sorry," said her mother.

"I can't," said Sophie. "I'm not."

"Look, Sophie," they said, "we know what Dawn did. The boys told us."

Sophie waited.

"I'm sure she didn't mean to," said her mother.

"It was only a woodlouse," said her father, "after all."

A Bad Back

Sophie was walking round the garden, wearing a pair of her mother's very old sunglasses. They were very dark glasses with a white frame. They made Sophie look like a panda. They made pink flowers look red and yellow flowers look golden and cabbages look blue.

Sophie walked along the path that ran along the front of the house and peered in through the dining-room window. Inside, everything looked very dark, the dining table, the chairs, the dresser with its rows of plates. The wood-block floor, usually the colour of milk chocolate, had turned to plain. But whatever in the world was that long shadowy thing lying on the floor?

"Yikes!" shouted Sophie. "It's a dead body!" and she galloped off down the path and through the back door and into the kitchen.

"Mum!" she cried. "There's a dead body on the dining-room floor."

"A dead body?" said her mother, busy stirring something. "I hope not, Sophie. But you're right. There is a body on the dining-room floor."

"Whose?" said Sophie in a strangled voice.

Her mother turned from the cooker.

"Goodness me!" she said. "You look like a panda. Take those things off. No wonder you couldn't recognize your own father."

In the dining room Sophie's father lay flat on the hard wood-block floor, his arms by his sides, and stared gloomily at the ceiling.

Sophie peeped round the door.

"Daddy?" she said.

"Yes."

"Are you all right?"

"No."

"What's the matter?"

"My back hurts."

"I'm not surprised," said Sophie. "Lying on that hard old floor. If you wanted to have a rest, why didn't you go to bed?"

Sophie's father sighed.

"It's not because I'm lying on the floor that my back hurts," he said. "It's because my back hurts that I'm lying on the floor."

"Oh," said Sophie. She walked across the room and stood, feet apart, hands on hips, staring down at her father's upturned face with a worried frown on her own. "What have you done to your back?" she said.

"I don't know," said her father in a grumpy voice. "All I did was bend down to pick up a newspaper and something went *click*."

"And it hurt?"

"It certainly did."

"Does it now?"

"It's OK as long as I keep still and flat like this. It's the best thing to do, they say, but it's pretty boring."

Sophie lay down beside her father, her arms by her sides, and stared thoughtfully at the ceiling.

"Would you like to play a game?" she said.

"Not if there's any moving about in it."

"No," said Sophie. "We can play I Spy. You'll only need to move your eyes. That won't hurt your back. Playing I Spy will take your mind off it."

"Oh, all right," said her father. "You start."

"I spy," said Sophie, "with my little eye, something beginning with … *s*."

Sophie's father swivelled his eyes around the room. There was a row of saucers on the dresser.

"Saucer," he said.

"No."

He looked at the hanging light.

"Shade," he said.

"No."

On the wall there were pictures.

"Seaside," he said.

"You mustn't cheat, Daddy," said Sophie severely. "You can't see the seaside. It's miles and miles away."

"Yes, I can. In that picture."

"Oh. No, it's not that."

"I give up."

"You can't," said Sophie. "You can't just give up. But I'll give you a hint if you like."

"Go on then."

"Look above your head."

Sophie's father stared upwards.

"All I can see is the ceiling," he said.

"I knew you'd get it," said Sophie, "if you kept trying."

"Actually, Sophie," said her father, "*ceiling* begins with a *c*."

"How silly of it," said Sophie. "Well, then it doesn't count. It's my turn again."

Half an hour later Sophie's mother came in.

"Oh, I see you're being looked after,"

she said. "Perhaps you'll be a nurse when you grow up, Sophie."

"You know I'm going to be a lady farmer. Go on, Daddy, it's your turn."

"What are you playing?" said her mother.

"We're playing I Spy," said Sophie. "I'm winning."

"I think you've won," said her father hollowly. "We've spied every single thing in the room. Why don't you run out in the garden now?"

"Oh no," said Sophie. "It's much more fun playing with you. I know lots more games. I'll just go and get some things." And she plodded off.

Sophie's mother smiled.

"Poor old chap," she said. "You're a prisoner. You can't escape."

"I don't know how much more play I can stand," said Sophie's father.

"You'll just have to take it all lying down," said Sophie's mother. "The longer you can stay there, the better." And she went out just as Sophie returned with her arms full. She was carrying paper and pencils, a draughts board and a box of draughts, a pack of cards and a set of Happy Families.

"There!" said Sophie, dumping them all beside her father.
"That'll do for a start."

"I can't play all those games," said her father desperately. "Not when I'm lying flat."

"You can hold things in your hands, can't you?" said Sophie.

"I suppose so."

"Right. Here's a pencil and paper then. We'll begin with Noughts and Crosses."

At the end of a long, long morning, Sophie's mother came in again.

Sophie was sitting cross-legged beside her father. On her face was a look of triumph.

"Please can I have Miss Bun the Baker's Daughter?" she said. "And Master Bones the Butcher's Son?"

She pointed at the one remaining card.

"You," she said, "must be Doctor Dose the Doctor."

Wearily her father handed over Doctor Dose. His face wore a look of great suffering.

"Is it your back?" Sophie's mother said. "Is it worse?"

Sophie's father moved his head from side to side on the floor.

"No," he said. "I haven't had time to think about it."

"We've had loads of games," Sophie said. "I won nearly all of them."

"Go and wash your hands for lunch, Sophie," her mother said and, when Sophie had gone out, "How are you going to manage? Can you eat down there? The doctor should be here soon. Hadn't you better stay there till he comes?"

"I ... am ... not ... staying ... one ... minute ... longer," said Sophie's father.

Very carefully, he levered himself to his feet.

Very gingerly, he took a couple of steps towards the door.

"It does feel better," he said in a tone of surprise.

"I told you so, Daddy," said Sophie, coming back. "I told you playing games would take your mind off it."

In the middle of lunch the doorbell rang. Sophie answered it. It was the doctor.

"Hello," she said. "Is your name Dose?"

"Dose?" said the doctor. "No, it's Macdonald."

"Oh," said Sophie. "Well, come in anyway."

"What's this I hear?" said the doctor, coming into the dining room. "Trouble in this happy family? Done your back in, have you?"

"It feels a lot better now," said Sophie's father.

"Does it?" said the doctor. "Well, I can tell you one thing for sure, before I even have a look at you. There's only one way to deal with a bad back."

"There is?" said Sophie's father.

"Yes. The moment you've finished lunch, you lie down flat on it, on this nice hard wooden floor, and you stay there the rest of the day."

He turned to Sophie.

"You'll keep Daddy company, won't you?" he said. "Perhaps you could think of some games to play."

Such an Intelligent Look

It was September and the twins had just gone back to school. Next term Sophie would be going too. She thought about this and wondered if she would like it. There would be Good Things and Bad Things about Going to School.

The Bad Things would be:

1. Having to wear School Uniform.

2. Having to meet Dawn again, for Dawn was starting this very term.

3. Having to meet other Strange

Children, as awful as Dawn.

4. Having to meet strange Grown-ups; the Teachers might be awful too; Matthew and Mark said that they weren't, but you could never tell.

5. Having to eat School Lunches, especially pilchards in tomato sauce.

Of course there would be Good Things too, thought Sophie.

1. Not having to help wash up the breakfast things at home.

2. Being with her brothers in term time. (She did not know that once she was at school they would not take the slightest notice of her.)

3. Drinking Morning Milk: At home Mum always said, "If you're thirsty, have a drink of water – milk's fattening," but Sophie knew at school you were encouraged to drink your Morning Milk and sometimes there were extra bottles if children were away.

4. Doing Judo: Sophie fancied throwing someone down – Dawn perhaps.

5. Farming Lessons: You went to school, Sophie knew, to be taught things for when you were grown-up. They would say, "What are you going to be?" and she'd say, "A lady farmer," and then they'd give her Farming Lessons.

Sophie's present farming was carried out in the potting-shed. Here she kept her flocks and herds.

She had a new system of free-range woodlouse farming. She had given up collecting matchsticks, which they didn't much seem to like, and now kept the woodlice in a seed tray so that they could

come and go as they pleased, and fed them
on cornflakes; the cornflakes seemed to
disappear though she had never actually
seen a woodlouse chewing one.

This morning there were only three
woodlice in the seed tray, and
one of those was lying upside
down, its seven pairs of legs
pointed at the roof of the potting-shed.

"I hope *you* haven't hurt your back, my
dear," said Sophie, grinning as she tipped
it the right way up. She dropped a couple
of cornflakes into the tray.

"I wonder where the rest of the herd
has got to?" she said.

On a country holiday Sophie had once
seen a farmer calling in his dairy herd
for milking. "Cow! Cow! Cow!" he had
shouted, and the big black-and-white

84

animals had all started walking across the field towards him.

"Louse! Louse! Louse!" Sophie shouted, but nobody came so she ate the rest of the handful of cornflakes. She went on to inspect the rest of her stock in their various pens on an old table in the shed.

First there was a shoe box. On it was written SENTIPEEDS. There were two in it, one large and dark, one small and ginger. Sophie was planning to increase the size of this flock, but wild centipedes were difficult animals to capture, so quickly did they scuttle. She was not sure what they ate and was trying them with biscuit crumbs.

"These shouldn't upset you, my dears," she said. "They're digestives."

Next, there was an old cake tin full of soil and earthworms. Earthworms ate earth, Sophie knew, so there were no feeding problems here. She was only really interested in the largest worms, and measured her captures with an old wooden ruler. This was difficult, because it takes two people to stretch out a wriggling worm and she needed Matthew or Mark to hold one end. Her record to date was a giant of fifteen centimetres.

Beyond the worm tin was another shoe box marked YEAR WIGS. Earwig-keeping was a branch of Sophie's farming that she had only recently taken up, thanks to her great-great-aunt.

Before Aunt Al's visit, Sophie had been wary of these dangerous-looking beasts with their crescent-shaped nippers.

"They bite," she had said.

"Load of rubbish," Aunt Al had said. "No good being scared of animals if you're going to be a farmer. Go and catch one and bring it here." And Sophie had caught one (cautiously, using an empty matchbox as a trap), and Aunt Al had picked it out and it hadn't bitten her.

"You have to be firm with them," she had said. "Don't stand any nonsense."

So now Sophie collected earwigs (still using the matchbox), and fed them on fruit. She dropped a rotten plum into the box before moving on to a coffee jar, on whose glass wall hung a single enormous slug. It was dark brown in colour, with a

lovely orange
rim around
its huge sticky
foot. Sophie put a bit of cabbage leaf
into the jar. She was quite proud of this
monster, whose capture had covered her
hands in a thick slime that took pumice
stone to get off.

But her favourite animals were in the
last pen of all, a large cardboard box, and
she opened the lid of this and tore up the
rest of the cabbage
leaf and
dropped it
in. Under the
black printed
lettering on
the side of the box
(which said BAKED BEANS) was a single

word in big red capital letters (which said SNALES).

Ever since the day of the Great Snail Race, Sophie had become especially fond of these creatures. She would spend ages watching them crawl along in their dignified way, wiggling their stalky eyes and leaving glistening silvery trails on the potting-shed table.

Every day Sophie would go on a snail hunt around the garden, adding to her herd, and there were seldom fewer than twenty in the box, of all shapes and sizes and shades of green or brown. The number varied, because Sophie had cut a lot of snail-sized holes in the lid of the large box so that anyone who wished could leave.

But always in the back of Sophie's mind – as she turned over stones or peered into cracks in the garden wall or searched in the flowerbeds – was the hope that one day, perhaps she just might meet again one very particular snail.

"What did you have for lunch?" Sophie asked the twins when they came home from school.

"Pilchards in tomato sauce," they said.

Sophie's face fell.

"Did you see Dawn?" she said.

"Yes," said Matthew. "She's got a new pony."

"A blue one," said Mark.

"Were there lots of Strange Children?"

"Lots."

"Very strange."

Sophie tried a couple of Good Things.

"Did you do judo?" she said.

"Only juniors do judo," they said.

"Well, did you have Farming Lessons?"

Matthew and Mark looked at each other, and each rolled his eyes upwards and raised his eyebrows and tapped his forehead with one finger.

Gloomily, Sophie stumped off.

But after that, the day improved.

First, she found a large earwig and actually caught it with her bare hands. Then she found a very pretty caterpillar which she put into a small box in the potting-shed. She was not too sure how to spell it, so she simply wrote CAT on the box.

Good luck comes in threes, thought Sophie that evening as she gazed out of her bedroom window. It was a beautiful September evening. No one could possibly have been unhappy on such an evening, not even faced with pilchards in tomato sauce.

Sophie leaned on the sill and played with a little tendril that was trying to creep across it unnoticed. She looked straight down the creeper-covered wall and there, right under her nose and climbing up towards it, was a very small snail, a snail no bigger than Sophie's middle fingernail, a snail that was a lovely buttercup yellow.

Very slowly (but very determinedly) it plodded up the last few inches of wall and over the edge of the windowsill. Then it stopped and raised its head in greeting. It had such an intelligent look.

Sophie's face lit up in one enormous grin.

"Good evening, my dear," she said softly. "What took you so long?"

Collect all 6 stories about Sophie and her animal friends!

Sophie's Snail
DICK KING-SMITH
Illustrated by Hannah Shaw

Sophie's Tom
DICK KING-SMITH
Illustrated by Hannah Shaw

Sophie Hits Six
DICK KING-SMITH
Illustrated by Hannah Shaw

Sophie in the Saddle
DICK KING-SMITH
Illustrated by Hannah Shaw

Sophie is Seven
DICK KING-SMITH
Illustrated by Hannah Shaw

Sophie's Lucky
DICK KING-SMITH
Illustrated by Hannah Shaw

Dick King-Smith (1922–2011) is one of the world's best loved children's book authors. He won the *Guardian* Children's Fiction Prize for *The Sheep-Pig* (filmed as *Babe*), was named Children's Book Author of the Year in 1991 and received the 1995 Children's Book Award for *Harriet's Hare*. His fiction titles for Walker include the much-loved Sophie series, *The Finger-Eater*, *Aristotle*, *The Twin Giants*, *Lady Lollipop* and *Clever Lollipop*. For more information, visit:
www.dickkingsmith.com

Hannah Shaw has created a number of critically acclaimed and award-winning children's books, including *Evil Weasel*, which won the Cambridgeshire Children's Picture Book Award; more recently she has written and illustrated her own fiction series, *Stan Stinky*.

Of this project, she says, "I loved Dick King-Smith's books as a child and read the Sophie series to my younger sister – who used to be quite a lot like Sophie! I was excited to have the chance to put my own stamp on a great character and her adventures." Hannah currently lives in Stroud, Gloucestershire. Visit her website at:
www.hannahshawillustrator.co.uk